KU-345-461

Schools Library and Information Services
S00000686820

A Brave Spaceboy

Dana Kessimakis Smith ☆ Laura Freeman

Jump at the Sun · Hyperion Books for Children / New York

I am a boy, a brave spaceboy
I dream of exploring the stars

THIS END UP

I'm fixin' up my rocket
So I can zoom to Mars

I have a suit, some real space gear
I'm covered head to toe

So I'll be safe and sound inside
Anywhere I go

I pop the hatch, the rocket door
We wave good-bye to our team

We climb on board, we buckle in
The engines smoke and steam

HEN

I'm commander-in-chief, the one in charge
My pilot will help me fly

The crowd counts down

We shoot into the sky!

We orbit Earth, we circle round
We speed through space to our mark

Over and over, our capsule turns . . .

At once, the sky goes dark

We look behind us,
we see our home
It slowly fades from view

It looks just like a marble
My favorite shade of blue

We push the buttons, we turn the knobs
Traveling day and night

We float around inside our ship
We eat and sleep in flight

"Mission control!" we call our team
"Mars is just ahead!"

The planet is an awesome sight
A plain of rocky red

We lower the rocket,
we land with skill

There’s silence all around

We write our names, we gather rocks
And plant flags in the ground

We snap a picture, “Cheese,” we say—
A spaceboy souvenir

We leave our footprints in the dirt
Brave astronauts were here!

We travel home, three cheers for us!
Our daring journey ends

I am a boy, a brave spaceboy
Who now has *two* best friends.

For Boston and Olivia, who mean the world to me
–D. K. S.

For Jimmy, Griffin, and Milo—my team
–L. F.

For information address Jump at the Sun, 114 Fifth Avenue, New York, New York 10011-5690.

Printed in Singapore
First Edition
1 3 5 7 9 10 8 6 4 2
This book is set in 20-point Cantoria.
Designed by Elizabeth Clark
Reinforced binding
Library of Congress Cataloging-in-Publication Data on file.
ISBN 0-7868-0933-7

Visit www.hyperionbooksforchildren.com